J FICTION W (NEW)

THE BALL HOGS

By Rich Wallace
for younger readers:

Sports Camp

Kickers:
   #1 The Ball Hogs
   #2 Fake Out
   #3 Benched
   #4 Game-Day Jitters

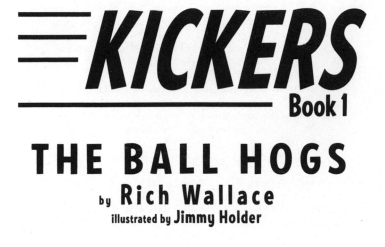

KICKERS

Book 1

THE BALL HOGS

by **Rich Wallace**

illustrated by **Jimmy Holder**

Alfred A. Knopf

New York

THIS IS A BORZOI BOOK PUBLISHED BY ALFRED A. KNOPF

Knopf, Borzoi Books, and the colophon are registered trademarks of Random House, Inc.

Visit us on the Web! www.randomhouse.com/kids

Educators and librarians, for a variety of teaching tools, visit us at www.randomhouse.com/teachers

Library of Congress Cataloging-in-Publication Data
Wallace, Rich.
Kickers : the ball hogs / Rich Wallace ; [illustrations by Jimmy Holder]. — 1st ed.
p.   cm.
Summary: Nine-year-old Ben, a natural athlete and member of the Bobcats co-ed soccer team, wants to overcome his inexperience and prove himself on the field, but his obnoxious teammate, Mark, keeps hogging the ball.
ISBN 978-0-375-85754-6 (trade) — ISBN 978-0-375-95754-3 (lib. bdg.) —
ISBN 978-0-375-89632-3 (e-book)
[1. Soccer—Fiction. 2. Teamwork (Sports)—Fiction. 3. Sportsmanship—Fiction.
4. Behavior—Fiction.] I. Holder, Jimmy, ill. II. Title. III. Title: Ball hogs.
PZ7.W15877Kib 2010
[Fic]—dc22
2009021349

The text of this book is set in 12-point Goudy.

Printed in the United States of America
June 2010
10 9 8 7 6 5 4 3 2 1
First Edition

THE BOBCATS

Team Roster

Ben

Mark

Erin

Shayna

Omar

Jordan

Darren

Kim

Coach Patty

CHAPTER ONE
Like a Real Player

"That kid is fast!" Ben said as a tall, thin boy ran across the soccer field.

"He sure is," said Erin. "I hope he's on our team."

"He must be," said Ben. "Why else would he be here?"

But Ben hoped that the kid was not on their team. He had seen him at recess during school. Ben knew the kid's name was Mark, and he was a pain, and bossy. Once he'd called Ben "brush head" after his mom had cut his hair.

But Ben liked his hair the new way. When it was longer, it would always get in his eyes.

Ben put his foot on top of his soccer ball and rolled it around. "Let's practice," he said. He gave the ball a kick and it rolled toward Erin.

Erin kicked at the ball, but it didn't go to Ben. It spun over to the side.

Ben ran toward the ball, but the tall kid got to it first. He stopped it with his foot and grinned at Ben. But Ben didn't like the way he was smiling. He looked tough. He was big for nine.

"Are you one of the Bobcats?" Mark asked.

"Yes," Ben said. "So is she." Ben nodded toward Erin, who was walking over.

"I hope you're good at dribbling," Mark said. "You're both kind of short. Especially her." Mark pointed at Erin. She was a few inches shorter than Mark, but she was a good athlete.

Ben stepped between Mark and Erin. "This is our first time playing on a soccer team," he said. "We don't know if we're good at it or not."

"Well, I'm good," Mark said. "I'll be the star of this team."

Ben looked at Erin and smiled. He felt nervous and didn't know what else to do. Practice hadn't even started yet, and Mark was already acting like a big shot.

A woman in a green T-shirt blew a whistle. "Over here, Bobcats," she said. "I'm your coach."

Eight kids ran toward the woman, who was carrying a net bag filled with soccer balls. "Have any of you ever played soccer?" she asked.

Several of the kids raised their hands.

"On a real team?" she asked.

Most of the kids put their hands down.

"That's okay," she said. "I've never coached a real team, either."

Mark's hand shot up again. "I was on a baseball team last summer," he said. "I was the best player."

"That's good," the woman said. "My name is Patty. I played soccer in high school, but that was a long time ago. We'll all have fun learning about the game together."

The Kickers League would include kids from all over town. Ben knew most of the players on his team from Kennedy Elementary School, but some of them went to Washington Elementary, on the other side of town.

Coach Patty opened the bag and handed out balls. Ben kept his own ball, which had been a present for his ninth birthday.

"Let's have a race," Coach said. "See that white line on the far end of the field? When I blow my whistle, we'll all run to that line. The winner is the one who gets there first, but you have to have your ball with you. And the only way you can move the ball is with your feet."

They set their soccer balls on the ground.

"I'll win by a mile," said Mark.

Patty blew the whistle. Ben kicked his ball and ran after it, trying to keep it in a straight

line. It wasn't easy. He kicked it a little more softly, then ran to it and kicked it again.

Mark was way ahead of the others. He had kicked his ball far up the field and was running after it at full speed.

Ben kept moving, kicking his ball a little at a time and then catching up to it. He knew he could run a lot faster, but it was tricky to keep the ball close to him.

Ben's last kick left the ball just over the

line. He pulled it back with one foot and stood on the line as the others came running up.

"Looks like you're the winner," Coach Patty said to Ben.

"He is not!" said Mark. "I was much faster than he was."

"But your ball went so far past the line that you had to chase after it," Patty said. "The point was to keep the ball with you."

Mark made a sour face and stared at Ben. "If it had been a real race, I would have won easily."

"Well, we're not here for a track meet," Coach said. "We're here to play soccer."

"I know that," Mark said. "You'll see. I'll be way better than that kid." He pointed at Ben.

Ben looked away. He wished more than ever that Mark was not on this team.

Ben wiped his forehead with his hand. He was starting to sweat from that running, and his heart was beating faster. That was a good feeling; it made him feel like an athlete. He took a deep breath and smelled the freshly cut grass.

There was a lot to like about soccer already. Everything except Mark.

For the rest of the afternoon, Coach had them work mostly on controlling the ball and passing. After practice, Ben and Erin started to walk home. They lived on the same block, just a few houses away from each other.

"Wait up!" yelled Mark.

Ben turned with a scowl. "What do you want?" he asked.

"I told you I'd be the best," Mark said.

"You weren't the best. There were a lot of good players here."

"Well, I was better than you," Mark said.

A car horn beeped, and Mark turned to look. "That's my mom," he said. "I'll see you twerps next time." And he ran off.

"He acts tough, doesn't he?" Erin said.

Ben just nodded. A guy like that could spoil all the fun this season.

Erin stopped walking and undid her shin guards. "These are a little uncomfortable," she said.

"I'm leaving mine on," Ben said. If anyone saw him walking home, he wanted them to know he was a soccer player. Of course, he was carrying his ball, too, but lots of kids had soccer balls. The shin guards made him look like a real player.

"You'll get used to them," Ben said.

"I hope so," said Erin. "I barely noticed them during practice, but they did start poking my skin after a while."

"Soccer players are *tough*," Ben said with a smile. "Can't let a little thing like a stinging shin stop us."

"Oh, sure, you're real tough," Erin said,

teasing. "Remember the other day when a spider was spinning a web from your bicycle to the fence? You had to get your brother to chase it off."

"It was a big spider," Ben said. He was a little embarrassed, but he laughed at himself anyway. "Maybe it was poisonous."

"It wasn't poisonous."

"Well, it was *big*," Ben said. "I thought Larry might want to study it. That's why I had him come out."

"Sure you did, Mr. Tough Guy."

"Larry wants to be a scientist."

"I'm sure he could find his own spiders to study if he wanted."

They were nearly home. Ben stopped walking and tossed his soccer ball into the air. As it came down, he tried to catch it on his thigh and bounce it again, but it fell off to the side. Ben had seen some high school kids practicing that type of juggling. Some of them could keep the ball in the air for several minutes at a time. That was a skill he was eager to learn, but it certainly wasn't easy.

They'd reached Erin's house. "I'll see you tomorrow at school," she said. "Don't let the spiders bite."

"Bye."

Spiders didn't really bother Ben very much. He *was* tough. At least he thought he was. Being around Mark today had made him feel sort of weak and puny. But he wouldn't let that get to him. He'd show Mark who was the better player.

CHAPTER TWO
Spoiling the Game

The next morning, Ben looked for Erin at school. He found her near the door, talking to a girl with a long dark ponytail. The girl had been at the Bobcats' practice.

"This is Shayna," Erin said.

"Hi, Shayna," Ben said. "How did you like soccer practice?"

"It was fun," Shayna said. "I liked playing goalie."

"Do you like our coach?" Ben asked.

Shayna giggled. "Yeah. She's my mother!"

Ben blushed. "I didn't know that."

"What did you think of that kid Mark?" Shayna asked.

Ben shrugged. "He was a jerk."

"He's in my class," Shayna said. "Nobody likes him."

"He sure likes himself," Ben said. "He thinks he's a big star."

"My mom will keep him in line," Shayna said. "She won't let him take over the team."

"That's good," Ben said. "He could ruin everything."

The school bell rang, so Ben and Erin waved to Shayna and walked toward their classroom.

"She's nice," Erin said.

"She'll be a good teammate," Ben said. "So we'll have at least *one* good one."

"Think we'll win any games?" Erin asked.

"I hope so. I practiced by myself last night."

Ben had loved soccer practice. When he got home, he had taken his ball into the yard and kicked it around for nearly an hour longer. He weaved around the swing set with it and pretended he was racing past players from another team. He kicked the ball against the garage door, and he learned to stop it with the inside of his foot.

After supper, Ben had written down some of

the things the coach had said at practice. He pinned the list to his bulletin board. He underlined the most important tip: *Always have fun!*

"Coach Patty said we should dribble every day," Erin said.

"I wish we had *practice* every day," Ben said.

"I know. We only have three practices before our first game. How will we ever learn everything we need to know?"

Ben shrugged. "I guess we won't. But most of the kids in the league are new, too. They won't be any better than us."

Ben took his seat in the classroom and looked around. Of all the other kids in the class, only Loop could beat him in a race. And only Tyler could jump as far. So he knew that he was a good athlete. Now he just needed to show that on the soccer field.

"Take out your spelling books," said Ben's teacher, Mrs. Soto.

Ben kept thinking about dribbling his soccer ball.

"Ben?" said Mrs. Soto. "Are you with us?"

So he took out his spelling book and tried to forget about soccer.

At recess, Ben usually played a game called four square with some kids from his class. He looked forward to it all morning. After reading and math and social studies, he was always ready to run around.

All four fourth-grade classes had recess at the same time. Other kids played tag or used the swings, and there were usually at least two games of four square going on.

Ben took his spot in the fourth square, where he'd been the previous day when recess ended. The fourth square was for the server— the place where each player wanted to be.

Reaching that square and holding on to it was the goal.

"Let's get going!" said Loop from square number three. "I'm ready to move up!"

"Better get used to that square," Ben said with a smile. "This one is mine."

Loop's real name was Luis Pineda. Ben bounced the ball in his square and then hit it toward Tyler. Tyler let it bounce once and then knocked it toward Nigel.

Ben stayed ready, his arms spread slightly and his knees bent, waiting for the ball to return to him. He loved the suspense.

The ball darted around the squares, with each player hitting it skillfully. Ben knew this group was good—they might keep the ball moving for more than a minute before anyone bobbled it or knocked it out of bounds.

But Loop fooled Ben by hitting a very soft volley into his square. Ben was ready for a firmer shot and didn't put much muscle into his return. The ball landed directly on the line, and Ben was out.

Loop jumped across the line into the fourth square, and the others moved up one space. Ben shook his head and stepped out, waiting

on the side as another player moved into the first square.

"Tough break," said Ryan, who was next in line.

"Don't worry about me," Ben said. "I'll have the fourth square back before recess ends."

Ben looked around the playground. Kids were running around in the field next to the playground, playing tag or having races. A shout made Ben look back at the four-square game.

"That was in!" Tyler yelled.

"It was *out*!" Loop shouted back.

"You must be blind." Tyler pointed at Ben. "In or out?" he asked.

Any player on the sideline was expected to act as a judge when there was a dispute. But Ben hadn't been paying attention.

"I didn't see it," he said.

"How about it, Ryan?" Tyler asked.

"I thought it was out," said Ryan.

"Then you're blind, too," Tyler responded.

"It's two against one," Ben said. "Loop and Ryan said it was out."

Tyler glared at Ben, but he stepped out of the square to the sideline. Tyler was one of the bigger fourth graders. He was competitive, but he usually stayed calm. "That was in," he said as the game started again.

"Get over it," Ben replied. He frowned and watched the game more closely. He'd be the next one in.

"Loop's always cheating," Tyler said.

"No, he isn't."

"Easy for you to say," Tyler said. He ran his hand through his curly brown hair and wiped some sweat on his shirt. "Loop cheats when he thinks he can get away with it. He thinks every close call should go his way."

"I haven't seen him cheat."

"Well, he just did. The ball I hit was in." Tyler looked down at the pavement, then scowled at Ben. "I'm starting a new group. You can stay in this one if you want, but I've had it with Loop."

Tyler walked away, but no one else wanted to start a new four-square group. He joined the other one instead. Nigel went with him, so that group now had seven players, and Ben's group had just four.

With six or seven players, there was more pressure to hold on to a square. But with only four, no one was ever really "out." They just kept moving from square to square.

"This stinks," Ryan said after a few minutes. "I might join that other group tomorrow if we can't get any more players."

"Me too," said Irvin.

"Then you'll have too many," Ben said. "Four square's no fun with eight or nine players either. You spend half the time just standing on the side."

"We need to make a deal," Loop said. "Get

some of those players to switch to our game. We'll see how much Tyler likes it when that group's down to four."

"It was fine the way it was," Ben said. "We always had five or six, and so did they."

"Maybe we can recruit somebody else," Irvin said.

Ben looked around. He saw Mark from his soccer team out on the grass, yelling and running. He certainly didn't want Mark in this game.

A few of the other kids on the playground had tried four square before, but Ben knew that the better players were already in one of the groups. Tyler was one of the best players—he was a sharp hitter and very quick—and Ben wanted him back, even if he was a complainer.

He glanced at Loop, another great player. Tyler and Loop had argued before, but usually the fights ended quickly. This time their feud was spoiling things for everybody. Everybody in this group, at least. The other game was thriving.

"I'll talk to Tyler later," Ben said. "Let's play."

"I don't feel like it," Loop said. He walked over to a swing and sat down, pumping his legs to get going.

"Me either," said Ryan.

Ben picked up the ball and bounced it hard. He caught it in one hand and shook his head. That was it for today. There was a spelling test right after recess, but Ben still wanted to play. He watched the other four-square game for a minute from several feet away, then leaned against the brick wall of the school and waited for recess to end.

CHAPTER THREE
Broken Rules

"Who wants to play a game of soccer?" Coach Patty asked as the kids gathered on the sideline for a break.

"Me!" said Ben, raising his hand in excitement. All of the others did the same thing. The Bobcats were midway through their second practice and they hadn't expected to scrimmage yet.

So far today, they'd worked on passing the

ball with the inside of their feet instead of their toes, and they'd done a lot of dribbling. Coach had shown them how to do a "throw-in," tossing the ball onto the field to get the game restarted when it went out of bounds.

Coach set up some orange cones on both ends of the small field. Those would be the goals. She pointed to Erin, Ben, Shayna, and a boy named Jordan and said, "You're one team." She waved her hand at the other four players—Mark, Omar, Kim, and Darren. "And you're the other. Four against four. Let's see what you've got!"

Ben ran to the center of the field and jumped up and down. He couldn't wait to kick that ball.

"Looks like you're all set, Ben," Coach said. "We'll leave you at forward for the start." She put Erin up front, too, and told Jordan to play defense and Shayna to start as goalie.

"But the defensive player should be part of the offense, too," Coach said. "And the forwards have to help out on defense. All of the players on a side should work together. Pass the ball and let each other know you're there to help."

But when the game began, the players forgot right away about their teammates. They ran around in a swarm, kicking at the ball and chasing it and not even trying to pass.

Ben got his foot on the ball, but another player knocked it away. When Erin took possession, Ben and all the others ran toward her.

"Move away!" Erin shouted to Ben. "Get open for a pass."

Ben moved away, but the swarm of opponents got to Erin before she could pass. They kicked the ball away and the entire group moved toward the goal, where Shayna was standing.

Jordan finally stuck his foot into the mob and knocked the ball the other way, and the whole group started moving toward the other goal.

Ben ran over, too. He got in front of one of his opponents and kicked the ball to the side, and everyone chased after it.

But the ball went out of bounds.

Mark ran over to it and picked it up, then ran back to the sideline. He kept both feet on the ground, brought the ball over his head with both hands, and threw it, just as Coach Patty had demonstrated. But instead of throwing it toward a teammate, he threw it down the field toward the goal.

With Mark's speed, he was the first player to get to the ball. He kicked it hard and ran after it, but Coach Patty blew her whistle and everyone stopped.

"Good throw, Mark," she said. "But the rule

is that the thrower can't be the first one to touch the ball after it hits the field. You have to throw it to a teammate."

"But I'm the best one!" Mark said.

"We'll see about that," Coach said. "But a rule is a rule. Let's try it again."

"Wait a minute!" said Ben. "If he broke the rule, then shouldn't my team get the ball?"

"Good point," Coach said. "But maybe Mark didn't realize what the rule is. Let's give him another chance, since this is practice."

This time Mark threw the ball hard at his teammate Omar. The ball bounced off Omar's shin guard and back toward Mark, who kicked it up the field.

"Was *that* legal?" Ben called to Coach.

"It was legal, but not very sportsmanlike," Coach said.

Ben chased after Mark. The ball was several feet ahead of him, but there was no one between Mark and the goal. Mark reached the ball, kicked it forward again, and chased after it. He was getting very close to the goal.

Ben was running at full speed and had nearly caught up to Mark. He could see that Mark was close enough to shoot. Shayna was crouched in front of the goal, but Mark would be hammering that ball any second.

Ben caught Mark and inched past him, then slid toward the ball with his leg extended. Mark tripped over Ben's leg and flew forward, landing face-down on the grass as Shayna ran up and kicked the ball away.

The whistle blew sharply and everyone stopped. Ben jumped up from the grass and smiled. He'd stopped Mark from scoring!

But Coach was not happy. "That was very dangerous, Ben. And illegal," she said. "No tripping allowed. You both could have been hurt."

"But I stopped him!" Ben said.

"Doesn't matter. A referee could toss you out of the game for a risky move like that."

Mark was on his feet now, too. He bent over and rubbed his knee, then hobbled around a bit.

"Are you okay?" Coach asked.

"Yeah," Mark said. He glared at Ben. "I would have scored if he hadn't cheated."

"I wasn't cheating!" Ben said. He turned to the coach and spoke softer. "I didn't know that was illegal."

Nothing made Ben feel worse than being accused of cheating. He knew he had made a rough play, but he hadn't meant to break a rule. "Sorry," he said.

"Well," Coach said, "if everyone's all right, then get started again. Mark gets a free kick from the spot of the foul."

"Can I kick it into the goal?" Mark asked.

"Yes, since you were fouled."

Mark took about five steps back, then ran toward the ball and kicked it hard. It lifted into the air and flew far past the goal, but it was too wide. Shayna trotted over and retrieved the ball, then kicked it back into play.

Erin ran to the ball and began dribbling up the field. Ben ran in the same direction, trying to get open. Then he felt a shove and stumbled, hitting the ground with his hands and pushing back up.

When he looked around, he saw Mark running toward Erin. Mark glanced back and gave Ben a mean smile. Ben ran toward the swarm of players.

"Spread out!" called Coach.

But spreading out hadn't done much good for Ben. No one was able to pass the ball with all those players around. The only way he'd get it was to take it away.

As the game continued, Ben kicked at the ball several times, but no one was able to dribble it for more than a step or two. So neither team came close to scoring. After several more minutes, Coach blew her whistle again.

"Let's switch positions," she said. "The goalies and defensive players move up to forward; the forwards drop back." Coach smiled. "No one except the goalies has even

33

tried to stay in a position yet. Let's think about that. Try to move the ball as a team, passing and moving and talking to each other."

Erin walked over to the goal and Ben moved into the center of the backfield as his team's defender. He was sweaty and his breath was fast, but he was ready for more action. He noticed that Mark was playing defense for the other side, so they'd still be working against each other. Omar had taken over as goalie.

"I've said this ten times already, but think about it," Coach said. "Spread out. Don't swarm all over the ball. If you have the ball, move it forward and find a teammate to pass to. If you don't have the ball, either play defense or get open."

Ben decided to give it a try. He hadn't had any luck trying to beat the swarm; maybe Coach's strategy would work.

So Ben stayed back on defense, about

halfway between Erin and the center of the field. The ball went toward the opponents' goal with five kids after it, then came back Ben's way as Mark took possession and booted it up the field.

Back and forth went the swarm. Then, with the players near the sideline about halfway up the field, Shayna took possession and began to dribble. The entire middle of the field between Ben and the other goal was wide open.

Ben began sprinting up the field, yelling at Shayna to pass. Shayna kicked it hard across the field. The ball was well in front of Ben, but he was closest to it. Mark wasn't playing defense like he was supposed to; he was part of the swarm. So if Ben could get to the ball, there would be no one between him and the goal except Omar.

Ben pumped his arms and ran as hard as he could. He was eight feet ahead of the swarm and about thirty feet from the goal when he reached the ball. He tapped it with his right foot, then his left, then slowed just enough to allow himself to plant his left foot and kick the ball with all his might toward the goal.

Omar lunged for the ball and managed to get his hand on it. The ball bounced to the side, missing the goal but staying on the field. Ben was the first to reach it. He pivoted toward the goal, but the swarm was on him now.

Shayna was open, but Ben shot the ball again. It hit Mark in the leg and flew in the opposite direction.

Again the players chased after it in a mob. This time Ben was with them. Up and down the field they ran, never quite getting near either goal again. Ben's strategy had almost worked. By getting open he'd come closest to scoring a goal.

But he hadn't scored. Nobody had. They'd

been scrimmaging for half an hour and the score was 0–0.

Practice was just about over. They'd only have one more session before their first real game.

Coach Patty blew her whistle and clapped her hands. "Great job today," she said. "Nice hustle."

But Ben wasn't happy. He was worried about this team.

How would they ever win a game if they couldn't even score a goal in practice?

CHAPTER FOUR
A Wasted Recess

When Ben reached his desk the next morning, he found a folded note tucked inside.

JOIN OUR NEW FOUR SQUARE GROUP! Meet at the court near the swings as soon as recess starts. Nigel, Irvin, Ryan, and Elliott are in, plus me. Room for one more. Will it be you?

—Tyler

There wasn't much "new" about the group, except that Loop was being excluded and Elliott was taking his place. They'd even be using the same court they always used.

Ben looked over at Tyler, who was turned in his seat to face Elliott, seated behind him. Tyler caught Ben's eye and gave him a serious nod.

Loop was standing in the back of the room, joking around with Erin and another girl. He probably had no idea what Tyler was trying to do.

Not fair, Ben thought. But he certainly didn't want to waste another recess, so maybe he'd have to join Tyler's game after all. He figured Loop could always join the other group.

Ben read the note again. Then he glanced at the clock: 8:29. Class would start in one minute. He'd have a couple of hours to decide what to do before recess.

Joining Tyler would be the easy thing to do, but it didn't seem right. Keeping Loop out would be like saying that he had cheated. There was a difference between cheating and just trying too hard. Like that illegal move Ben had made in soccer practice. He hadn't meant to break the rule.

Maybe he and Loop should start *another*

new group. But what fun would that be if none of the other good players were with them?

The bell rang for the start of class. Ben crumpled up the note and tossed it into the back of his desk.

"Are you joining us?" Tyler asked as they hustled outside for recess.

Ben shrugged. "Not today," he said.

"Why not?"

"I just don't feel like it."

Tyler made a face. "Suit yourself."

Ben took a seat on one of the swings. Tyler and his group started playing. Loop had joined the other group.

"Watch how high I can go," said Erin, who was on another swing.

"Not too high!" called one of the teachers.

Erin gave Ben a half-smile. "They always worry too much," she said.

Ben saw Mark on the playground, playing tag with some kids from his class. He was making a lot of noise.

"There's the big shot," Ben said.

Erin laughed. "At least he always plays hard," she said. "He'd be really good if he used his brain, too."

"I don't think he's learned anything," Ben said. "He made the same mistakes in our second practice as he did in the first one."

"We all made mistakes," Erin said.

"Some make more than others."

"There's Shayna!" Erin said. She waved to Shayna and called her over.

"Hey, team," Shayna said. "My mom says we need to work on our passing."

"That's true," Ben said.

"She says our two best players are our two

worst passers," Shayna said. "It's not that you can't pass, it's that you don't."

Ben nodded. Shayna meant him and Mark. Ben knew she was right.

As recess ended, Mark came running up to them. He was sweating from the game of tag. He stared at Ben. "How come you're hanging out with girls?" he asked.

"Because I didn't play four square today," Ben said.

"You should have played tag with us," Mark said. "I beat everybody."

"How do you beat everybody at tag?" Ben asked.

"I don't know," Mark said. "I just did. When I was 'It,' I tagged somebody else. When I wasn't 'It,' I kept away."

"That's what everybody does," Ben said.

"I did it better."

Ben shook his head. *This guy is too much*, he thought.

Back in class, Ben tried to concentrate on Mrs. Soto's math lesson. But his mind kept going back to the soccer field. He knew that the best chance the Bobcats had to win a game would be if he and Mark could somehow work together.

But how could you work with someone who never thought about anyone else? Mark never passed and he always made harsh comments when Ben made mistakes.

I guess I'm not perfect either, Ben thought.

CHAPTER FIVE
The Opening Game

The sun was warm and bright as Ben's team lined up for its first soccer game. They were all wearing blue shirts that said BOBCATS.

Across the field, the Tigers were ready to play, too. They had orange shirts. There were eight teams in the town league, and the Bobcats would play each of them at least once over the next two months. The best teams would earn spots in the play-offs, and the winners of the championship would get trophies.

"There'll be six players on the field for each team—three forwards, two defenders, and a goalie," Coach Patty said. She explained that each game would include two twenty-minute halves. "So all eight of you will play a lot."

Ben, Erin, and Mark were in the front line for the Bobcats. Shayna was the goalie, and Kim and Darren were on defense.

The whistle blew and a Tiger player kicked the ball hard. All of the players ran after it. Mark got to it first.

"Over here!" called Ben. But Mark kicked the ball up the field and chased it.

Coach Patty had reminded the team not to crowd around the ball.

"If your teammate has the ball, go to a place where he or she can pass it to you," she'd said.

So Ben ran toward the front of the goal.

Mark kept racing up the field, kicking the ball
again. Three Tigers were running close to him.
Mark was almost at the end of the field.

"I'm open!" yelled Ben. He had reached a
place just in front of the Tigers' goal. If Mark
would pass the ball, Ben would have a chance
to score.

But Mark had kicked the ball too hard. It
rolled over the line at the end of the field before he could catch up to it. The referee blew
his whistle.

"That's out of bounds," the referee said. "The ball goes to the Tigers."

Ben and Erin and Mark jogged back toward the center of the field.

"I was open," Ben said to Mark.

"So was I," Mark said.

"I was right in front of the goal," Ben said. "You made a dumb play."

Mark just looked away.

Ben shook his head. The Tigers were coming toward the Bobcats' goal. A swarm of blue and orange shirts ran over, trying to get the ball.

The game went back and forth for several minutes. Once again, Mark dribbled the ball all the way down the field. Ben and Erin ran to the front of the Tigers' goal.

Mark tripped over the ball and fell down.

While Mark was getting up, one of the Tigers moved quickly down the field with the ball. Then she made a pass right across the front of the Bobcats' goal. A teammate was waiting there. He stopped the pass with his foot, then shot it hard toward the goal.

Shayna was ready. She dived toward the ball, but didn't quite reach it. The ball flew into the net. The Tigers had scored!

"Remember to pass the ball," Coach Patty told the team during a break. "We're Bobcats, not hogs. We won't score if one player hogs the ball."

Ben shook his head. He knew who Coach was talking about.

Coach put Ben on defense for a little while, and later he played goalie. He stopped one shot that made his hands sting, and he was proud that the Tigers didn't score against him.

Late in the game, Ben, Shayna, and Mark were on the front line. The Tigers still had a 1–0 lead.

"Let's tie this game!" Ben shouted as Shayna ran up the field with the ball.

Two Tigers ran close to Shayna. She stopped and made a nice pass to Mark.

Mark booted the ball and ran after it at full speed. When he reached it, he kicked it again and kept running.

Ben was running, too. He got close to the goal and darted to the left. "Pass!" he yelled to Mark.

Mark turned toward the goal and tried to squeeze through two Tigers. One of them kicked the ball away. Another Tiger booted it far down the field.

While the players were chasing the ball, the referee blew his whistle. "Game's over!" he called.

The Bobcats had lost, 1–0.

Ben was breathing hard and he was sweating. He walked to the side of the field with his teammates. Coach Patty clapped her hands.

"Great game!" Coach said. "You guys really played hard."

They shook hands with the Tigers, then joined their coach again.

"We should have won," Mark said.

"Maybe next time," Coach said.

Maybe, Ben thought. *But only if Mark learns to pass the ball. We'll never win if we don't play like a team.*

He decided to add *Pass the ball!* to the list of soccer tips he was keeping.

Later that day, Ben sat at the kitchen table across from Erin, staring at the chessboard. He had just four players left, but Erin had six. Even so, Ben thought he had a good chance to win.

He moved his black rook forward and captured one of Erin's white pawns.

"Got ya," he said.

"Nice move," Erin said with a frown. But

then she smiled. "I think you overlooked something, though."

Erin picked up her bishop and Ben winced. She slid the piece across the board and captured Ben's rook. "Looks like someone's in trouble," she said.

Ben rubbed his chin with his hand and

studied the board. Erin was right. There was no way he could win now.

"Give up?" Erin asked.

Ben shook his head slowly. He moved his pawn forward one space. "It's not over yet," he said.

But Erin moved her bishop again, putting Ben's king in danger. It only took two more moves for her to win.

"Nice try," she said.

Ben had never beaten Erin at chess. She'd taught him how to play a few months before. Erin had been playing with her dad for two years. She always managed to capture Ben's stronger pieces, especially after he'd taken one of her weaker ones.

"It's like a soccer game, isn't it?" Ben said. "You have to know where all of the players are and what they're able to do."

"That's true," Erin said. "You always have to be thinking ahead. And if one of the players makes a risky move, it usually hurts the whole team."

"Like Mark, huh?"

Erin laughed. "Yes. Like Mark."

Erin picked up one of the black rooks. "See, this player can move up and down the board as far as he wants. But if he tries to win the game all alone, he'll usually get knocked out. The pieces have to work together."

"You'd be a good coach," Ben said.

"Thanks."

Ben's parents came into the kitchen.

"Time to chop the broccoli!" Dad said. He winked at Erin. "Ben's favorite food."

Ben winced. "Better cover it with tomato sauce," he said.

"It'll be garlic and olive oil," Mom said. "We just bought some shrimp at the market."

"Fresh pasta, too," Dad said. "Can you stay for dinner, Erin?"

Erin looked at the clock. "I have to go

home. It's my dad's turn to cook tonight. He's roasting a chicken."

"Okay," Ben said. "Maybe tomorrow we can play chess again. I think I'm getting closer to beating you."

"In your dreams," Erin said.

Ben walked to Erin's driveway with her, then turned back. He started to run, imagining that he was racing past soccer players and heading toward the goal. He dodged left, then right, and saw himself shooting the ball into the net.

The pieces have to work together, he thought.

He'd be ready to score if that pass ever came.

CHAPTER SIX
Tough Competition

Tyler's new four-square group was still going strong. They'd asked Ben to join for the first few days, but he'd refused to play unless they let Loop back in, too. Now they didn't bother asking.

Ben hadn't played four square in a week. And now Loop had dropped out of the second group because the action wasn't fast enough. He and Ben just tossed their ball against the brick wall and took turns catching it.

"Aren't we the two best players?" Loop asked.

"Probably," Ben said.

"So why are we the only ones not playing?"

Ben shrugged. He pointed to the second group. "They've already got six." He jutted his chin toward Tyler and the others. "And they've got an attitude problem."

"Well, this is boring. Some kids from another class asked me if I wanted to start a third group."

"Really?" Ben asked. "Who?"

Loop pointed across the playground. "That guy, for one."

Ben couldn't believe Loop was pointing to Mark. "*Him?*"

"Yeah."

"He's a total pain."

"He's a good athlete," Loop said. "He was on my baseball team last summer. So what if he's a pain?"

"He's on my soccer team," Ben said. "Believe me, we won't have any fun playing with him."

"Too bad," Loop said. "We still have time to get a game going before recess is over. You in?"

"No thanks." Ben sat against the wall. Soon there were three games under way. Sixteen players were involved.

But not Ben. He tried to act as if he didn't care that he was sitting there alone, but it was hard to keep his eyes off the four-square games. Loop had joined right in with Mark and that group, and they seemed to be having a good time. Tyler's group had the best players, but Ben could have had fun in any of the games.

As they walked back to class, Ben grabbed Loop by the arm. "The only reason I wasn't in

Tyler's group was because I was standing up for *you*."

"Well, I got tired of wasting time," Loop said, pushing Ben's hand away. "All Tyler wants to do is argue. If you want to go back, go ahead."

Now Ben felt a push from the other side, too. "Don't bother," Tyler said. "We don't want either one of you back."

Ben stopped walking. "Who do you think you're shoving?" he asked.

Tyler took a step closer. "I *think* I'm shoving you."

"Well, watch it."

"What's the matter, Ben?" Tyler said. "Wouldn't they let you in the baby game either?"

"What baby game?"

"Loop's baby four-square game. Did they leave you out, too?"

Ben clenched his fists and glared at Tyler. But Loop stepped between them. "It's a better game than yours," he said.

"It is not."

Mr. Kane, who taught one of the other fourth-grade classes, was coming toward them quickly. "Is there a problem here?" he asked sternly.

Ben stared at Tyler. "No problem," he said.

"It *looked* like a problem," Mr. Kane said.

"It wasn't," Loop replied, but he was giving Ben an angry look. "We were just talking about four square."

"Then get back to class," Mr. Kane said. They were the last ones on the walkway between the playground and the school. Mr. Kane held the door open and the three boys walked in. Then the teacher went one way and Ben and the others went the other toward their classroom.

So Ben and Tyler and Loop were alone in the hall.

"You already had your chance to join us," Tyler said to Ben.

"Who says I want to?"

"You did."

"No, I didn't," Ben said. "I said I didn't because of Loop."

"So you *would* have joined us."

"*Would* have. Won't now."

"We don't want you."

"Big deal." Ben walked faster to get away from Loop and Tyler. How did he end up like this when he'd just been trying to stick up for Loop? This had totally backfired. He entered the classroom and took his seat.

The three of them glared back and forth at each other for the rest of the morning.

At lunch, Ben found a table in the corner and ate quietly. Erin walked by and asked him what was wrong.

"Nothing."

"Oh, sure," she said. "You're sitting by yourself and you think you can tell me nothing's wrong?"

"I'm fine," Ben said. "I just feel like being alone."

Erin shrugged and joined a group at another table.

Ben wasn't alone for long. Loop walked over and took the seat across from him. "What's the idea of getting mad at me?" Loop asked. "You could have played if you wanted. I'll fight my own battles with Tyler. I don't need your help."

Ben stared at his sandwich. He'd only eaten half of it. "I belong with the best players."

"You mean Tyler's group?"

"Whichever group is best. Definitely not with that kid Mark."

"He seems okay to me," Loop said. "Listen, you can sit on the swings and feel sorry for yourself or you can join our group on Monday. I'm playing."

Ben took a bite of his sandwich and looked away. "I'll think about it," he said.

"Don't strain your brain," Loop said. "Recess is supposed to mean we can stop thinking for a little while between classes."

CHAPTER SEVEN
A Second Chance?

It rained the day of the Bobcats' second game. Ben didn't mind. The grass was wet but the air was warm. He was excited. He knew that his nice blue shirt would get muddy, but that was part of the fun.

Coach Patty asked Ben to play goalie for the first part of the game.

Ben was quick and he was good at stopping shots. But the Rabbits had fast runners with strong legs. They took some hard shots.

Ben stopped two shots, but the third one got past him.

"Nice try!" called Kim.

"Good effort!" yelled Shayna.

"I would have stopped that!" shouted Mark.

At halftime, Coach Patty called the team over. "You're playing very well," she said. "We're only one goal behind. If we work hard, we should be able to tie this game."

Ben moved to the front line for the second half, eager to score. But Mark kept hogging the ball. He missed one shot and lost the ball two other times.

"Pass it!" Ben said. "Don't be so selfish."

Mark did not answer.

The score stayed 1–0 for a long time. The rain stopped but the field was slippery. It was hard to keep from falling.

Late in the game, Ben finally got the ball near the Rabbits' goal. A Rabbit player lost control near the sideline, and Ben was there to steal the ball. He dribbled up the field. *I can score*, he thought.

Ben ran closer to the goal, but some Rabbits were right with him. He was surrounded by purple shirts. The goalie was blocking his path, too.

Ben heard Mark yell, "I'm open!"

Ben looked quickly to his left. Mark was

near the goal, several yards away from Ben. A good pass would mean a goal for sure.

He never passes to me, Ben thought. *Why should I pass to him?*

Now three Rabbits were trying to take the ball from Ben. He turned and shifted and moved quickly away. His foot slipped on a muddy spot.

Mark was still open, but Ben shot the ball instead. The goalie easily stopped it.

"I was wide open!" Mark said as they ran back.

This time Ben just looked away.

Time ran out soon after that. The Bobcats had lost again.

Erin put her hand on Ben's shoulder. "Why didn't you pass to Mark?" she asked.

"He never passes to me," Ben said.

"That's the problem, isn't it?" she said. "You just made it worse."

Ben kicked at the mud. "I thought I could score."

"It doesn't matter who scores," Erin said. "A goal is a goal. We would have tied the game if you passed."

Ben frowned. He wiped his hands on his shirt and let out his breath. He looked down at his feet. His socks and shin guards were spotted with mud.

Across the field, the Rabbits were jumping up and down and cheering.

It must feel great to win, Ben thought.

He was beginning to wonder if he would ever find out.

Ben pulled his sweatshirt on over his head and took a seat on the bench. Loop's team had run onto the field, warming up for the next game.

Ben felt as if the loss was his fault. He had been the goalie when the Rabbits scored. And he had decided not to pass the ball when Mark was open near the goal.

So it didn't make him feel any better when Mark walked over.

Mark was holding a small bottle of juice. That reminded Ben that he was very thirsty.

"I would have scored if you'd passed the ball," Mark said.

"I took a good shot," Ben said.

"They stopped it easy," Mark said with a frown. "I was the one with the clear shot. No way they would have stopped me."

"They stopped you earlier!"

"That's because my foot slipped!" Mark said. "It was muddy out there."

"My foot slipped, too," Ben said.

"That's why you should have passed."

"You would have missed the shot anyway!" Ben turned and looked toward the parking lot. His mom and dad were talking to Coach

Patty. They all were laughing and smiling. They didn't seem to care that the Bobcats had lost.

Ben looked back at Mark. Mark made a fist and held it up.

"You'd better pass next time," Mark said.

Ben swallowed hard. "You'd better pass, too," he mumbled. Then he walked toward the parking lot.

I'll never *pass to that guy,* Ben thought. *Not in a million years.*

"Here's the soccer star," Dad said, rubbing Ben's wet hair.

"Great game," Mom said. "You were awesome."

Ben rolled his eyes. He knew he wasn't a star. And he knew he hadn't been awesome. He'd played hard and done some good things, but he'd made a lot of mistakes, too.

"I was all right, I guess," he said. "But we should have won. Or at least tied."

"Your coach said she's very happy with how hard you work," Dad said. "Now let's get you into some dry clothes and have lunch."

"You've got plenty of games left," Mom said.

"You'll start winning. I was so excited when you took that last shot."

Ben's brother, Larry, patted him on the shoulder. "I was sure that shot was going in," he said.

Ben nodded, but he knew better. That shot had no chance.

He wished he could do it over again. But would he shoot the ball harder or pass it to Mark?

He wasn't sure what he would do. But he knew the chance would come again. There were many games left to play.

Mom handed him a plastic bottle filled with lemonade. Ben unscrewed the lid and fished out a couple of ice cubes. He popped them into his mouth.

He wished he could play another soccer game right now. But he'd have to wait a whole week.

He had a new soccer tip to add to his list: *Be a supportive teammate*.

That might be the hardest one for him to stick to. At least when it came to playing with Mark.

CHAPTER EIGHT
Back in the Loop

"So, what's the decision?" Loop asked as Ben took his seat in the classroom on Monday morning. "Are you with us or not?"

Ben frowned. He hadn't decided what to do about recess. "We'll see," he said.

Ben knew one thing. He *would* be playing four square. A week on the sidelines had been more than enough. He just wasn't sure which group he'd be joining.

If he walked up to Tyler's group and waited his turn, they'd probably take him back. But he'd be in for some tough talk first.

He was welcome to join Loop's game, but then he'd have to put up with Mark.

The third group would take him, but they had the weakest players.

"You can always play hopscotch instead," Loop said.

Ben scowled, but Loop just grinned. "I'm kidding," he said.

"Very funny."

"Maybe you can set up a game by yourself," Loop said. "You can jump back and forth in all four squares."

"Why would I do something that stupid?"

"Because you don't seem to be getting along with anybody else lately," Loop said. "You won't play with Tyler, you won't play with Mark. Get used to it, Ben, you're not the only one who wants to play. You don't get your way every time."

Ben was shocked. He had tried to be the peacemaker. Now they were all turning against him. Maybe he *would* just sit this out again. Who needed four square anyway?

Ben sat on the bottom rung of the monkey bars at the start of recess. Erin walked over.

"You're still moping around?" she asked.

"No."

"Oh, excuse me," she said. "I didn't notice how happy you are."

That made Ben smile, but he fought it back. "They're jerks," he said.

Erin glanced at the four-square games in progress. "Yeah," she said. "They could be having a lot more fun over here doing nothing, I suppose. Like you."

Ben nodded slowly.

"I'm joining Loop's game," Erin said. "They've only got four today." She made a tiny waving gesture with her fingers. "See you later."

Ben gripped the monkey bars tightly while she walked away. "Wait up," he said.

Erin grinned as Ben leaped up and joined her. As they reached the game, Ben noticed that Loop had a big smile, too.

"Look who's here," Mark said the next time the game stopped. He glared at Ben, and Ben glared back.

Erin stepped into the first square and Loop served the ball. Ben would be in next. He watched the action closely. Loop was the only one of these kids he'd played with regularly, so he wanted to see what skills they had.

Not bad, he thought as the ball flew from square to square. *This'll do for now.*

Ben couldn't help but notice that Mark was a pretty good player. That was hard to believe, because four square is a game where control makes a big difference. Relying on speed or strength isn't as effective as accurately placing the ball in another square.

Mark was always out of control on the soccer field, but he was showing some real patience here.

Erin made a nice save and directed the ball into Loop's square. Loop lunged for it but knocked it out of bounds. So Ben was finally in the game.

Loop held out his hand as he walked out of the square, and Ben smacked it. "Hope you're not too rusty," Loop said.

"Don't count on it," Ben said.

It was a warm day and Ben felt a surge of energy as he took his spot. He was diagonally across from Mark, who'd be serving.

"Don't get too comfortable," Mark said, giving Ben a nasty smile.

"Try me," Ben said.

Mark served the ball hard with a wicked spin, and it landed in Ben's square. Ben took a quick step back and brought his hand down at a sharp angle, slicing at the ball and catching it just right. The ball rocketed back into Mark's square and zipped past him.

"Lucky!" Mark said as he ran after the ball.

Ben stood tall and grinned at Erin. She rolled her eyes and shook her head, but she was smiling, too.

Mark frowned and tossed the ball to the next server. Then he stood alongside Loop as they waited for the next break in the action.

Ben quickly worked up a sweat, dodging around and making some excellent shots. Recess ended just as he reached the fourth square.

He pointed toward the pavement and said,

"This spot is *mine*, people. I'll see you all back here tomorrow."

"One serve," Mark said. "That's how long it'll take me to put you back on the sideline."

"We'll see about that," Ben replied. He walked away with his head held high.

A week without four square had been *way* too long.

CHAPTER NINE
Three Points

Ben was glad to get to practice that afternoon. He had thought about it all day. He couldn't wait to run.

He got to the field early, but he didn't want to wait until practice started. So he dropped his ball and started to kick it, working hard to keep it close to his feet. That was another tip on his list. He ran two laps around the outside of the soccer field. The ball only got away from him once.

He started to run a third lap. Suddenly he heard someone running close behind him. He turned and saw Mark.

Mark did not have a ball, so he was running very fast. He caught up to Ben and kicked Ben's ball to the side.

"Quit it!" Ben said.

"You're too slow!" Mark said. "And you

think you're so cool because you have your own ball." He kept running.

Ben ran over to his ball. He could see Coach Patty and Shayna getting out of their car. Other members of the team were arriving, too.

"Come over here!" Ben called to Mark.

"Why?"

"Just come here."

Mark stopped running and walked over to Ben. "What?" he asked.

Ben didn't want to admit this, but he had to say it. "We've been hurting the team."

"I haven't."

"Yes, you have," Ben said. "When we don't pass, we hurt the team's chances."

"I'm the best player we have," Mark said. "You hurt the team when you don't pass to me."

"You do the same thing when you don't pass to me!"

Before Mark could answer, Coach Patty

called the team over to her. "We've really improved," she said. "If we work hard today, I think we'll be ready to win on Saturday."

Coach had the team do some drills that focused on passing. "It's the best way to set up a shot," she said.

In one drill, a player would take the ball to the corner of the field, then pass backward to a teammate. That player then passed the ball across the field, sending it right in front of the goal. A third player was waiting there to stop the ball, then shoot it into the net.

"Think of a triangle," Coach said. "The ball moves from one point, to a second point, to a third point. The defenders will chase after the ball. If we pass it quickly, we'll have an open shot before they can catch up."

They worked through the drill several times.

"Now it will get harder," Coach said. "We'll

do the same drill, but with a defender on the field. We'll have to speed it up."

Ben waited on the field for Erin's pass to come from the corner. He stopped the ball and turned quickly toward the center of the field. Mark was playing defense. He came toward Ben, trying to stop him. Ben swiftly kicked the ball toward Kim.

Kim took the pass, dribbled once, and shot the ball into the goal.

"Great job!" Coach said. "Good things happen when we work together."

Ben jogged over to the spot in front of the goal. It was his turn to be the third point in the triangle.

Here came the pass. Ben stopped it with the inside of his foot. He took a step to his left to get past the defender. The only thing between him and the goal was the goalie.

He planted his left foot and kicked hard with his right. The ball left the ground and flew on a line drive toward the goal.

The goalie reached for the ball, but it landed solidly in the net. Ben had scored. He lifted his arms and yelled, "Yes!"

"Nice shot," Coach Patty said. "That's how teamwork pays off."

After practice, the team gathered around the coach again.

"Passing is the best way to move the ball," she said. "But if you have a good chance to shoot, then take it. The second point of the triangle doesn't always have to pass. Sometimes that player has a chance to score, too. And the third point doesn't always have the best shot, either. He can pass the ball right back."

Ben wiped his sweaty face on the sleeve of his T-shirt. There was no doubt that the team had played better today.

Now if they could only manage to do it in a game.

CHAPTER TEN
Holding His Ground

The next day at recess, Ben was back on the four-square court. The ball came into Ben's square and he controlled it skillfully, letting it bounce once before slamming it toward Loop.

Loop stepped back and swatted the ball across to Mark, who spun it into Ben's square.

Ben pivoted and sent the ball back at Mark, who bobbled it and knocked it out of play.

Ben raised his fist as Mark chased after the

ball. "Fourth square," he said proudly. He'd held that position for several rounds.

"Sorry," Mark said, bouncing the ball as he walked back to the game. He didn't *sound* sorry. "You palmed the ball."

"What?"

"You heard me. That was an illegal shot."

"No way," Ben said. He shifted his eyes from Mark to Loop to Erin.

Erin shook her head. "Too close to call."

"Looked good to me," Loop said, "but he's got the right to call a foul."

Ben frowned, but he said, "Okay." He stepped out of the square and the others moved up. Another kid from Mark's class took over the first square.

No big deal, Ben thought. *I'll be back in soon.* He was sure he hadn't gripped the ball with his palm. He was way too experienced for that. He wasn't going to let Mark drag him into an argument, though. He remembered what Loop had said about not expecting to get his way every time.

Within a minute, Ben was back in the first square, determined to reclaim the server's position before the end of recess.

Back and forth the ball flew, with lots of

94

chatter coming from the players. This was turning out to be a pretty good group. *Tyler can have his dumb game*, Ben decided. *Who needs 'em?*

Ben moved up to the second square, then the third. He glanced at his teacher, Mrs. Soto, who was standing near the swings and checking her watch. Recess was just about over.

Mark served the ball and Loop fired it across to Erin. Ben stayed ready, his eyes fixed on the ball as it flew from square to square. *Mark's going out*, he thought. *He'll pay for that bogus palming call.*

The ball came his way, but the shot forced him toward the back of his square; it'd be too tight a shot to try to send it to Mark. So Ben lobbed the ball into Erin's square, and she easily knocked it to Loop.

This time Loop's shot set Ben up perfectly. He leaned back, turned his hand quickly, and swiped at the ball. It darted toward the far edge of Mark's square and took a hard bounce. Mark lunged for it but barely got his hand on it as it rocketed out of the square.

Ben took a big step into the fourth square, but Mark said, "No way!"

"Yes, way!"

"That was a double hit."

"Get out. It was clean."

"It was not!" Mark stepped into the square, too, face to face with Ben.

Mark was several inches taller than Ben and certainly stronger. But Ben held his ground.

"You're gonna call a foul every time I knock you out?" Ben asked.

"If it *is* a foul."

"That wasn't!"

Mark pressed the ball against Ben's chest and pushed. Ben lifted his hand to Mark's shoulder and pushed back. Mark's face turned red and he stepped out of the square.

"What's going on?" called Mrs. Soto, walking over quickly.

"He's being a baby," Mark said. His voice was shaky.

Ben was steaming mad, but he laughed. He could tell that Mark was backing down. "Mark calls a foul every time I outplay him."

The other games had stopped and everyone had gathered around Ben and Mark, expecting a fight.

"Recess is over," Mrs. Soto said. "Everyone line up." She looked at Ben, then at Mark. "Except you two."

She stood with her hands on her hips. "Who isn't playing fair?" she asked.

"Him," said Mark.

"Him," said Ben.

Mrs. Soto let out a sigh and smiled gently. "Maybe you two should be in different games tomorrow."

Great, Ben thought. *I have to change games again?* "He says I did a double hit."

"Did you?"

"No."

Ben noticed that Mark was looking down at the pavement and biting his lip. He seemed to be afraid of Ben's teacher.

"Ben sounds pretty sure," Mrs. Soto said. "Is he mistaken, or are you?"

Mark shrugged. "I don't know," he said, kicking softly at a pebble.

"Think you can try again tomorrow?" she asked.

"All right by me," Ben said.

Mark looked away. "Sure."

"I'll be watching," she said. "Play fair or find a different group. And if I see any fighting, you'll both be staying in for recess for at least a week."

Mrs. Soto clapped her hands and addressed

the rest of the students. "Inside," she said. "Orderly."

Ben sneered at Mark, but Mark wasn't looking. So Ben followed him to the door. When they reached it, Mark turned and muttered, "Baby."

Ben didn't respond. But he felt stronger somehow, and not afraid of Mark anymore. He'd stood up to him and Mark had backed down.

Ben would be in the fourth square tomorrow. He knew Mark wouldn't try to claim it. And even if he did, Ben would definitely hold his ground.

CHAPTER ELEVEN
Breaking a Sweat

The Bobcats' next game was against the Sharks. The Sharks had won both of their games this season. It would be a hard test.

The sun was shining brightly as Ben sat on the grass, watching the Eagles battle Loop's team, the Falcons. Ben would be out on that field in a few minutes.

His teammates were also waiting, either watching the game as Ben was or kicking a ball around off to the side. Ben was well aware that Mark hadn't arrived yet.

Maybe he won't show up, Ben thought. Part of him hoped that would happen. He and Erin and Shayna were more than ready to work together, and Mark would keep hogging the ball. But Ben also had to admit that Mark was a pretty good athlete. He *could* be a big plus, if he'd show some teamwork. Otherwise, he did more harm than good.

The other game ended. Loop's team had lost, and he looked frustrated.

Ben jogged onto the field, then sprinted from one end to the other. He couldn't wait to get started.

Coach Patty was standing by one of the goals. She waved her arm and the Bobcats ran over.

"I only see seven," Coach said. "Who's missing?"

"Take a guess," said Shayna, rolling her eyes.

"Well, let's hope he gets here soon," Coach said.

Ben turned to Erin. "Let's hope *not*," he whispered.

"I'll play goalie for the warm-up," Coach said. "Give me a passing line and a shooting line."

Ben took the first spot in the shooting line, about ten yards in front of the goal. Jordan took the ball toward the corner and passed to Ben, who fired it toward the goal.

Coach grabbed the shot and rolled it to the corner, where Erin was waiting. "Keep it moving!" Coach yelled. "Quick passes, quick shots. Everybody keep running."

Ben took the next pass and sent a sharp pass to the shooter. Then he angled over to the shooter's position, bobbing up and down as he waited. He was already starting to sweat. Things were looking good for the Bobcats; everybody seemed ready.

After Ben shot, he ran to the corner. And there was Mark, just ahead of him in line. He hadn't seen him arrive.

Mark turned and smirked at Ben, then looked away. He fielded the ball, kicked the ball hard toward the next shooter, and ran to that line, bumping Ben with his shoulder as he went by.

What a jerk, Ben thought. But that's what he'd expected. Mark was going to keep doing whatever was good for himself.

The Sharks were fast and talented. They kept control of the ball for most of the first half, and the Bobcats had to work hard to keep them from scoring.

Ben spent most of the half on defense. He stole the ball twice and forced one Shark to kick the ball out of bounds.

But the Sharks kept coming back. They took several hard shots. Finally, one of the shots got past Shayna, who was doing a great job as goalie. The Sharks had the lead, 1–0.

"Keep it up," Coach Patty said at halftime. "We'll put Ben and Mark and Shayna on the front line for the second half. Work together, and let's score some goals of our own."

Ben sat on the bench and took a drink of water. He glanced over at Mark, who had taken off one of his shoes and was rubbing his foot.

Ben hadn't spoken to Mark since the four-square game the other day. He wondered if Mark had thought about what Ben had said about passing after the last practice.

I'll find out soon, Ben thought.

The second half started out just like the first. The Sharks took the ball and headed toward the Bobcats' goal, making sharp passes and dribbling quickly.

Erin stepped toward the player with the ball and blocked his path. The Shark player tried to dodge past her, but Erin got her foot on the ball and knocked it away. She ran to it and kicked it up the field. Shayna was there to get it.

Shayna took a few quick steps, running near the sideline. Ben turned and ran to the middle of the field.

"I'm here!" he called to Shayna.

Shayna passed the ball ahead of Ben. He ran it down and took control. The field was wide open ahead of him.

Ben ran up the field with the ball. Shayna was on one side of him and Mark was on the other, each about ten yards away.

Now the Sharks had caught up. Two ran over to Ben, blocking his path and coming toward the ball. But Ben was quick. He stopped short and turned his body to protect the ball. Then he kicked it along the grass toward Mark.

The Bobcats were moving now. Three good passes had done the trick. Mark was getting closer to the goal.

But two Sharks had raced over, and Mark no longer had a clear path to the goal. He moved away from them, but now he was in the corner of the field.

Ben yelled, "Triangle!" He'd noticed that they were set up just like in the drill they ran in practice. Mark was in the corner. Ben was the second point. And Shayna was the third point, right in front of the goal.

But what did Mark do? He shot the ball at the goal. It had almost no chance to get there. The ball rolled out of bounds.

"He's hogging the ball again!" Ben said to Shayna as they ran back.

Shayna shook her head. "I know. We were both open."

Ben looked at Mark. "Pass it!" he yelled.

Mark looked at Ben. And instead of making a face or saying something mean, he did something Ben never expected. He blushed.

"I thought I could score," Mark said. He shook his head. Then he ran toward a Shark player who was dribbling quickly down the field.

Mark kicked the ball at the same time that the Shark did. The ball popped into the air and bounced toward the sideline.

The Shark player got to it first. He kicked it hard, but it came straight at Ben.

The ball was too high for Ben to kick it, but he knew what to do. As long as he didn't use his hands, he could stop the ball with any part of his body.

The ball was coming toward Ben's chest. He leaned back and tightened his muscles. The ball hit his chest and fell to the ground. Ben started running with it right away.

The Sharks were caught off guard. Ben had lots of room ahead. He ran straight toward the goal, moving as fast as he knew how.

Only the goalie had a chance to stop him now. Ben was almost to the goal. The goalie

stepped toward him with his arms spread wide.

It would be a tough shot to make, but Ben knew that he could slip the ball to the side of the goalie and get it into the goal. He saw a flash of blue on his right. It was Mark!

Ben leaned to his left, hoping the goalie would dodge to that side. He did.

Ben's choice was clear. He softly passed the ball to his right, just in front of Mark. That side of the goal was wide open. Mark booted the ball into the net.

Mark leaped into the air and shouted, "Yes!" He'd scored the Bobcats' first goal of the season. And even better than that, the game was tied.

"Nice pass!" Mark said.

Ben couldn't believe what he was hearing. "Nice shot," he replied.

They ran back to their end of the field.

There was still time. They could win this game.

Here came the Sharks. They weren't done yet, either.

"Play tough defense!" called Ben. "Let's get that ball back."

Two quick passes brought the ball close to the Bobcats' goal. It looked as if the Sharks would get off a shot, but Erin stepped in and stole the ball. She dribbled once and passed the ball to Shayna.

"Here we go!" shouted Ben.

Shayna passed to Ben, then ran up the field. Ben took two steps and fired the ball back to Shayna. He ran alongside her, several yards away.

There wasn't much time left in the game. This would be the Bobcats' last chance to win it. Shayna and Ben and Mark raced up the field. They had to get a shot off soon.

Shayna had the ball deep in the Sharks' end of the field. Ben drifted back a few feet and shouted, "Triangle!"

Shayna passed him the ball. Ben dribbled forward. He could shoot or he could pass. But he had to decide in a second.

Mark was covered. Ben's best option was to shoot. He planted his left foot and brought back his right. Two Sharks ran in front of him. Ben pulled the ball back and dodged to his left.

Shayna had run over and was moving toward the goal. Ben could be a hero and try to score. Instead he passed the ball to Shayna.

Shayna shot hard. The goalie put up his hands and dived for it. The ball smacked off his hands and bounced wildly in front of the goal.

Ben and the others charged toward it. Bob-cats and Sharks. Blue and yellow. Everyone wanted that ball.

Ben reached it first. There was no time to dribble. No time to pass. He swung his foot at the ball and watched as it floated toward the goal.

The goalie was still on his knees. He reached for the ball with all his might. But he couldn't quite get it.

Ben had scored!

Now Shayna had him in a bear hug, and even Mark was slapping him on the shoulder. The Shark goalie shut his eyes and kicked at the dirt. All of the Bobcats were yelling.

The Sharks put the ball back in play. They kicked it hard and ran down the field. They had to score or they'd lose.

Ben ran toward the Shark player with the ball. He couldn't let them tie this game. The player passed the ball across the field. Erin got to it first and kicked it hard and long.

The referee blew his whistle. The game was over.

Ben dropped to his knees and raised his arms into the air.

"We did it!" Kim shouted.

"Great passing!" said Mark, giving Shayna a fist bump and grinning.

"We beat the best team in the league!" said Erin.

"No," said Ben. "We *are* the best in the league. We just had to learn to play like a team."

Now he knew what winning was like. It was a wonderful feeling. Especially since they'd done it together.

Ben ran to his parents, who were standing near the sideline.

His mom was beaming. "Great shot!" she said.

Dad held up one hand for a high five, and Ben jumped to slap it.

"We need to celebrate," Ben said. "Can we go for pizza?"

"Sounds like a good plan," Dad said.

"We're back in business," Ben said as they walked toward the car. "Finally got that win!"

Ben heard his name and turned to look. Mark was standing about twenty feet away, waving him over.

"I'll be right back," Ben said to his parents, and he walked toward Mark.

Mark looked serious. "Are you playing four square on Monday?"

"Of course I am," Ben said.

Mark nodded. "Me too." He smiled slightly. "No more double hits?"

"No more cheap calls?"

"No." Mark jutted his chin toward the soccer field. "We were pretty good out there today. . . . I guess you aren't *such* a twerp after all."

"You bet we were good." Ben glanced toward his parents, then he turned back to Mark. "It's just like Coach keeps saying. Work

117

together. Even if you don't always like each other, I guess."

"I guess."

Ben put his hands on his hips. He stared at Mark for a second, then nodded. "So I'll see you at recess," he said. He started walking away, then stopped. "There's a long way to go in this season," he said. "Lots more soccer games."

"Think we can win 'em all?" Mark asked.

Ben shrugged. "I think we finally know how to. . . . That doesn't mean we'll win 'em."

"Keep practicing," Mark said.

"You too."

Ben thought of that first practice. He thought of those close losses. But most of all he thought about scoring that goal. And he wished the next game could be tomorrow.

BEN'S TOP TIPS FOR SOCCER PLAYERS

- Always warm up before a game or practice. Try some jogging and jumping jacks.

- Work on keeping the ball close to your feet when you dribble. Don't just kick it and chase it.

- Pass the ball! It's the best way to move it. After you pass, move to an open space so the ball can be passed back to you.

- Be a supportive teammate. Say positive things and encourage everyone to work hard.

- Always have fun!

RICH WALLACE is the acclaimed author of many books for young readers, including *Sports Camp*; *Perpetual Check*; *Wrestling Sturbridge*, an ALA Top Ten Best Book for Young Adults; *Shots on Goal*, a *Booklist* Top 10 Youth Sports Book; and the Winning Season series. He coached soccer for several years, beginning when his older son joined a team in kindergarten.

Rich Wallace lives in New Hampshire with his wife, author Sandra Neil Wallace. You can visit him on the Web at www.richwallacebooks.com.

Don't miss
Kickers #2: *Fake Out*

The Kickers soccer league is heating up, and Ben's team, the Bobcats, has two losses, one win, and one tie. Ben knows he can pull his team out of its slump and right into the league play-offs with his new move: the fake-out. He practices the tricky footwork every chance he gets. But every time he tries it on the field, he flubs up, loses the ball, and hurts his team. Meanwhile, everyone else is faking *him* out. Is Ben out of his league?

In his Kickers series, award-winning author Rich Wallace offers action-filled novels about the Bobcats, a fourth-grade town soccer team, and their bid for the league play-offs.

Also available:
Kickers #3: *Benched*
Kickers #4: *Game-Day Jitters*